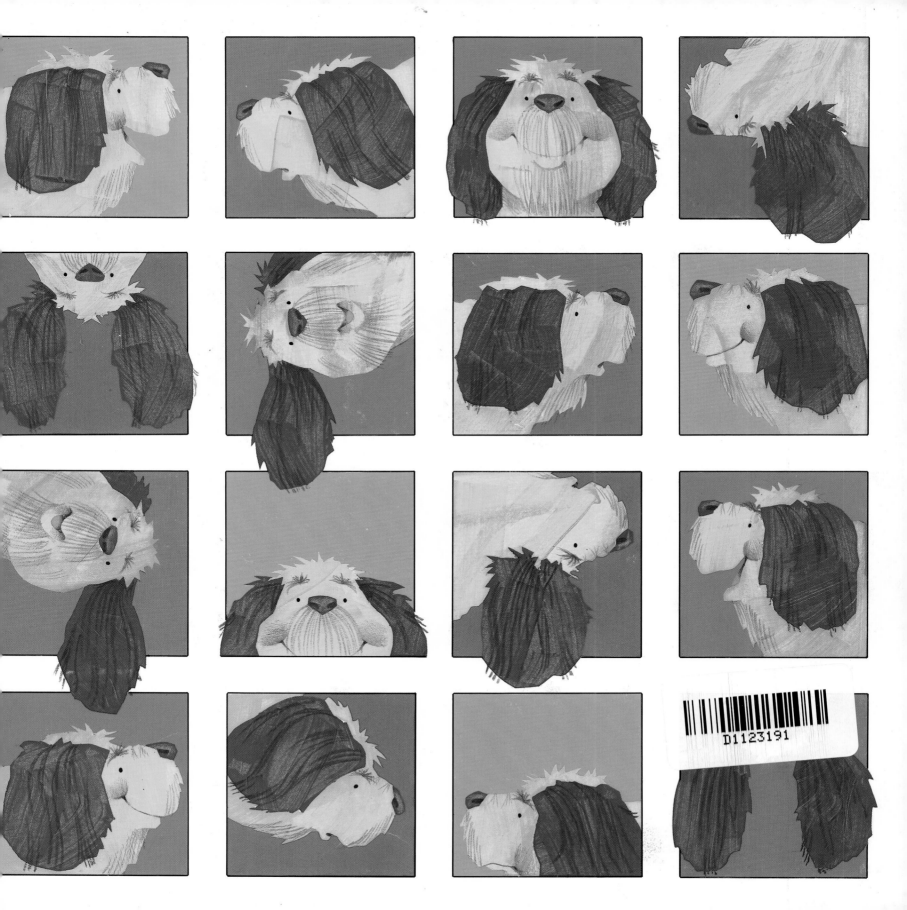

This edition published by Barnes & Noble, Inc.,
by arrangement with Brainwaves Limited
5 Highwood Ridge, Hatch Warren, Basingstoke,
Hampshire RG22 4UU, England.

1993 Barnes & Noble Books

ISBN 1 56619 283 8

Printed in Singapore by Tien Wah Press (Pte.) Ltd.
M 9 8 7 6 5 4 3 2 1

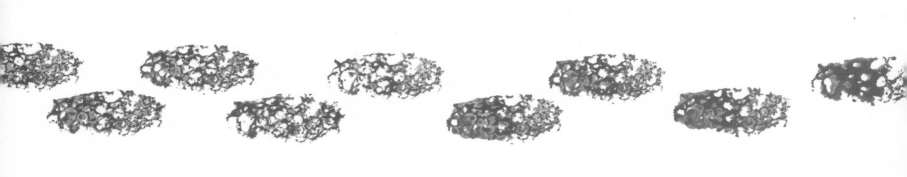

WHERE'S MY BED?

Written by Keith Faulkner

Illustrated by Jonathan Lambert

BARNES
&NOBLE
BOOKS
NEW YORK

The tired little puppy trotted into the kitchen. He felt like a nice long sleep in his warm, comfy bed.

But, when he got to the corner, where his bed usually was, it was nowhere to be seen.

So, the tired little puppy trotted off. he was going to look for another bed to sleep in.

He didn't see that his own bed had been washed and was hanging on the washing line outside.

so, off he went. . .

He peeped through a doorway and there was a very comfy looking bed.

"That looks warm and snug," said the tired little puppy. "I wonder if I can sleep in there?"

But, it looked too small.

Suddenly . . .

So, the tired little puppy went outside and down the lane. After a while he came to a pigsty and peeped over the wall.

Inside the pigsty was a small hut. "Perhaps I can sleep in there," said the tired little puppy.

But, it looked too muddy.

Suddenly . . .

So, the tired little puppy went on,
until he came to a henhouse.

Inside, there was a big pile of straw.
"I wonder if I can sleep here?" said
the tired little puppy.

But, it looked too prickly.

Suddenly . . .

So, the tired little puppy went on,
until he came to a pond.

There were reeds and rushes growing by
the waterside. "Perhaps I can sleep
here," said the tired little puppy.

But, it looked too wet.

Suddenly . . .

So, the tired little puppy went on, until he came to a tall tree.

He scrabbled up into the branches and found a cosy nest of twigs and dry grasses. "I wonder if I can sleep here," said the tired little puppy.

But, it looked too high.

Suddenly . . .

So the tired little puppy went on,
until he saw a dark hole in the
ground.

He peered inside to see a cosy burrow,
filled with soft grass. "Perhaps I can
sleep here," said the tired little puppy.

But, it was too narrow . . .

Suddenly . . .

So, the tired little puppy plodded slowly home again.

Inside, there was his very own bed. "I can sleep here now," yawned the tired little puppy.

And, it looked just right.

Suddenly . . .

"Out of that clean bed, with those muddy paws," said a voice. But, it was too late, the tired little puppy was already asleep!

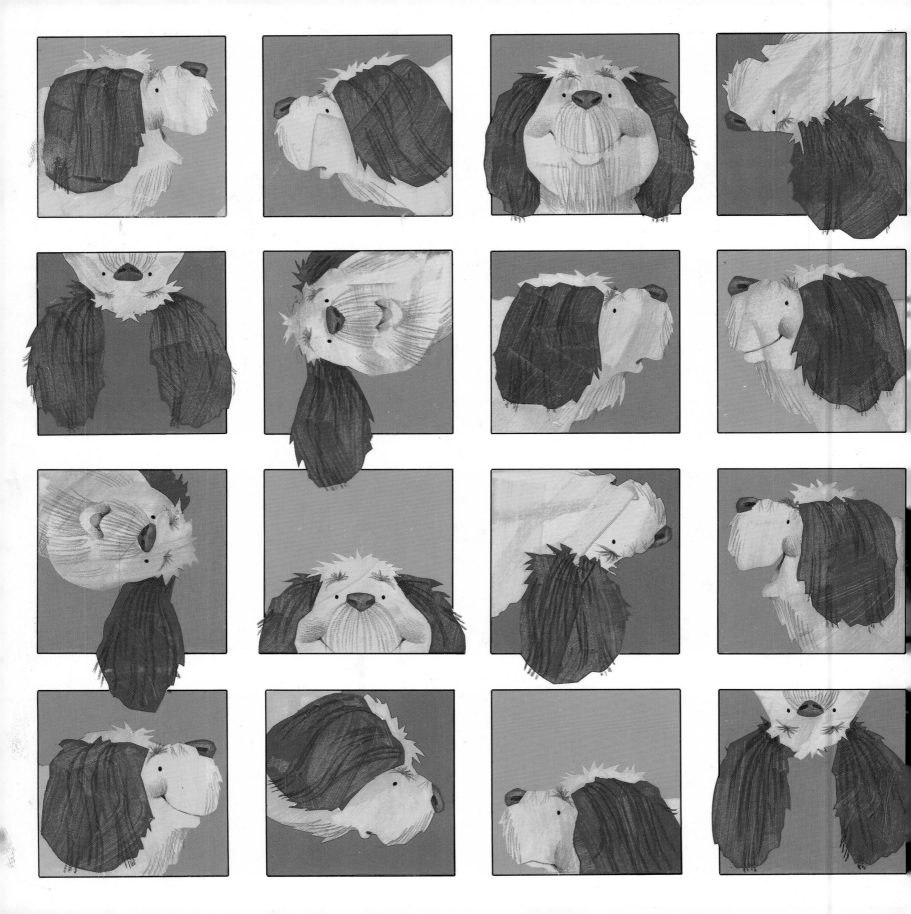